MY SUPER SCIENCE HEROES

MARIE CURIE AND THE POWER OF PERSISTENCE

words by
Karla Valenti

pictures by
Annalisa Beghelli

with
Micaela Crespo Quesada, PhD

sourcebooks
eXplore

TO ALL PEOPLE WHO BELIEVE IN AN ENDLESS POWER: THE POWER OF BEING
THEMSELVES, ABOVE ALL. AND TO MY FAMILY, MY EVERYDAY ENERGY AND LOVE.
—AB

TO MY FAVORITE SUPER HEROES: NICO, SOFIA, SANTIAGO, AND DAVE.
—KV

MARIE CURIE ALUMNI

Text © 2020 by Karla Valenti • Illustrations © 2020 by Annalisa Beghelli • Cover and internal design © 2020 by Sourcebooks
Sourcebooks and the colophon are registered trademarks of Sourcebooks. • All rights reserved. • Marie Curie Alumni logo design
is owned and licensed by the Marie Curie Alumni Association. • The full color art was created digitally. • Published by Sourcebooks
eXplore, an imprint of Sourcebooks Kids • P.O. Box 4410, Naperville, Illinois 60567-4410 • (630) 961-3900 • sourcebookskids.com
Library of Congress Cataloging-in-Publication Data is on file with the publisher. • Source of Production: 1010 Printing Asia Limited,
North Point, Hong Kong, China • Date of Production: December 2019 • Run Number: 5016620 • Printed and bound in China.
OGP 10 9 8 7 6 5 4 3 2 1

OOOH!

AHHHH!

OOOH!

Deep beneath an icy mountain, in a dark and craggy cave...

Super Evil Nemesis was reading his favorite book.

"Once upon a time, people didn't know anything, and that made them afraid."

"Ooooh!" the minions said.

"When people are afraid, they can be controlled," Nemesis went on.

"Ahhh!" the minions said.

"Step 1: Stop the spread of knowledge. That is how we shall take over the world! Bwah-ha-ha!"

The minions cheered and clapped.

Super Evil Nemesis did not know that at that very moment, brave heroes with their own brand of superpowers were being born all over the world.

And so begins our story: an epic adventure to save the world!

One cold and gray November morning in Poland, superhero Marie Curie was born. At the time, her name was Maria Skłodowska, and she didn't know she was a superhero. She didn't even know she had a superpower.

But she did.

ALERT!

Nov. 7, 1867—Maria Skłodowska is born in Warsaw, Poland. Her parents are teachers: Bronislawa and Wladyslaw Skłodowski. She has three sisters named Zofia, Bronya, and Helen, and a brother named Józef.

Nemesis called for one of his minions, Mr. Opposition.

"She must not be allowed to learn," Nemesis said. "Her ignorance will make her fearful and easy to control."

"An excellent plan," said Mr. O, and he went straight to work.

At first, Maria's goals were small, like her.

Maria didn't think Mr. O was very nice, but she wasn't about to let him stop her from figuring things out.

As young Maria grew, so did her search for knowledge. Her superpower grew as well.

ALERT!

Maria is an early reader and writer. She is a very bright student. (She even loves mathematics and physics!)

Nemesis was not happy, and Mr. O was forced to resort to more

After Maria's father lost his job, the family didn't have much money. That made it very difficult for Maria to concentrate on her studies.

Mr. O was certain this would defeat Maria.

It didn't.

ALERT!

June 1883—Maria is a star pupil and top of her class. She has completed high school and been awarded a gold medal!

"She must not be allowed to go on!" cried Nemesis.

"University is only for men and you are not a man," said Mr. O. "Your search for knowledge ends here."

"I will not give up!" Maria said, and she didn't.

ALERT!

Maria and her sisters are attending an underground school called the Floating University. The students meet in secret locations to study.

"Things are not at all going according to plan!" Nemesis groaned.

Mr. O agreed, especially because he could never find the secret locations.

When Maria completed her studies at the Floating University, Mr. O was waiting for her.

"To become a real scientist," he said, "you must work with **dozens** of other scientists and read **hundreds** of science books. You must do **thousands** of experiments in a laboratory!"

Mr. O was right.

"Girls in Poland are not allowed to do any of that. Ha! It's finally time for you to give up!"

Mr. O was right again. There were no more schools in Poland for Maria and her sister to attend. (Not even secret schools.)

But Maria's love of learning was no match for Mr. O.

"I will find a way! I will persist!"

ALERT!

Maria and her sister have made an agreement. Maria will work to earn money for Bronya to study in Paris. Later, Bronya will help pay for Maria to go to university.

"Noooo!" Nemesis cried. "My plan only works if she gives up!"

For seven years, Mr. O was as persistent as Maria.

When she worked as a teacher to earn money, he made sure she didn't get paid very much.

When she became a governess, he made sure she was so busy she didn't have time to study.

And when Maria still managed to study math and chemistry on her own, Mr. O did everything he could to stop her.

Eventually, Maria saved enough money to study at the University of Sorbonne in France.

ALERT!

November 1891—We're moving to Paris! Maria plans to study mathematics, physics, and chemistry.

I AM STARTING TO THINK YOU ARE NOT THE RIGHT MAN FOR THE JOB. ARE YOU SURE YOU CAN DO THIS?
—NEMESIS

YES I CAN! I WILL PERSIST!

Taking nothing more than some food, books, a folding chair, and a blanket, Maria (and sneaky Mr. O) left Poland for Paris. She moved in with her sister Bronya and took on the French version of her name: Marie.

Mr. O also took on the French version of his name: Monsieur O.

Their battle continued.

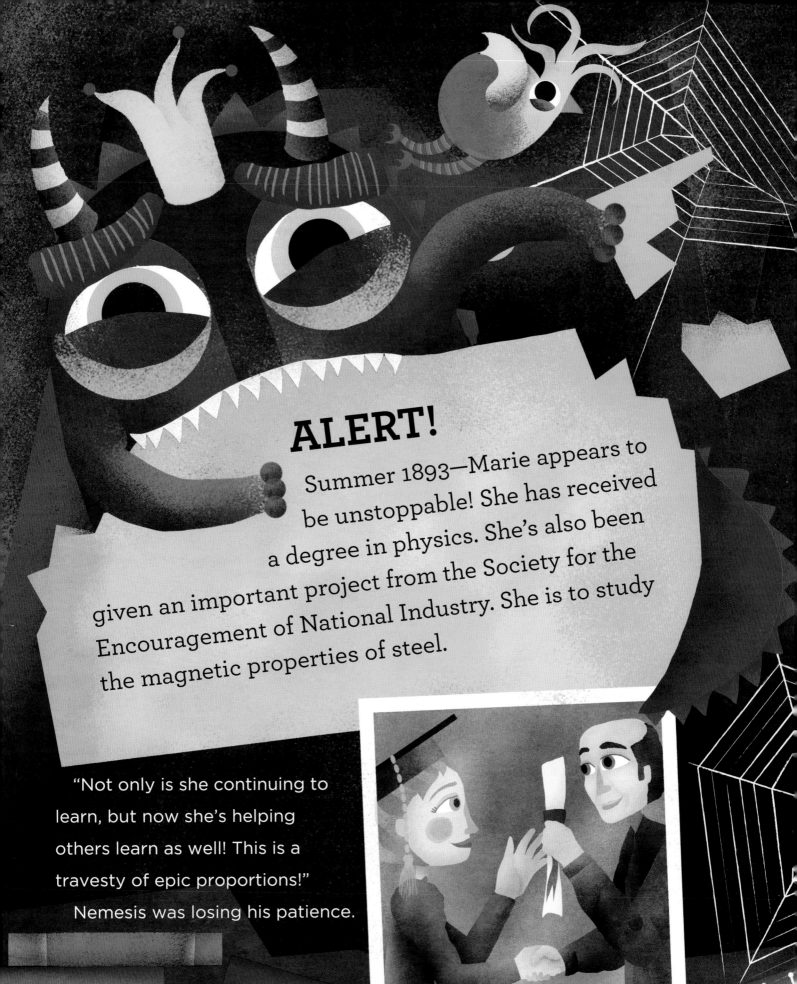

ALERT!

Summer 1893—Marie appears to be unstoppable! She has received a degree in physics. She's also been given an important project from the Society for the Encouragement of National Industry. She is to study the magnetic properties of steel.

"Not only is she continuing to learn, but now she's helping others learn as well! This is a travesty of epic proportions!" Nemesis was losing his patience.

Under the circumstances, Monsieur O thought it best not to tell Nemesis about Marie's second degree earned just one year later, this one in mathematics. Nor did he mention Marie's encounter with Pierre Curie, another Super Science Hero.

Pierre helped Marie find a laboratory where she could do her research.
They worked together on many experiments and became good friends.
In 1895, Marie married Pierre and they moved into a house together.
Monsieur O joined them.

Shortly after the Curies were married, a German physicist discovered rays that could move through objects and provide photo images of bones. The discovery of X-rays captured the attention of the scientific community (and of Monsieur O).

Around that time, uranium rays were also discovered. Marie was fascinated by their intensity and immediately began experimenting with them.

ALERT!

Marie has made an important scientific discovery: rays are a form of energy that comes from certain elements. They are a property of how the elements are made. Isn't that amazing? I'm sending some articles for you to read.

"I will call these elements *radioactive!*" said Marie.

Monsieur O quite liked the name.

"There's more," she went on. "Did you know? Certain compounds send out more rays than they should."

"They do?" asked Monsieur O.

"Why do you think that is?" she asked.

"I bet you'll figure it out!"

Monsieur O was right.

An unknown element inside those compounds was emitting powerful rays.

"But what is that element?" asked Monsieur O.

"I don't know yet," replied Marie.

"BUT I WILL FIND OUT!"

Marie and Pierre spent months experimenting in their laboratory.

Monsieur O never left their side (and sometimes even lent a hand).

Finally, Marie and Pierre found the answer: there were two secret elements—chemical elements called polonium and radium.

ALERT!

1903–Marie, Pierre, and Henri Becquerel (yet another Super Science Hero) were awarded a Nobel Prize in Physics for their discovery of radioactivity. Marie is the first woman ever to be awarded a Nobel Prize! Her research is going to help scientists learn more about physics, energy, atoms, and the human body. It's incredible!

"I bet you get another Nobel Prize," said Monsier O.
He was right.

In 1911, Marie received a second Nobel Prize, this time for her work in chemistry and her discovery of radium and polonium.

Marie Curie went on to achieve a great many things as a Super Science Hero, including:

• She was the first woman to become a professor at the University of Sorbonne in Paris.

• She became the head of the Radium Institute, a laboratory established for her to continue studying radioactivity.

• During World War I, she developed mobile radiography units that helped save the lives of many injured soldiers.

• She became a member of two very important science organizations: the International Commission for Intellectual Cooperation and the League of Nations.

Of all the things Marie Curie accomplished, the most important one of all was defeating Monsieur O, who eventually realized he was up against a superhero with a truly remarkable power:

PERSISTENCE

But, he didn't mind.

Nemesis, of course, was not so easily defeated. "As long as there is ignorance and people are afraid, I will prevail!"

But as every member of the League of Super Science Heroes knows,

KNOWLEDGE IS POWER!

You too can join the League of Super Science Heroes. Here are some facts to help you build up your own superpowers.

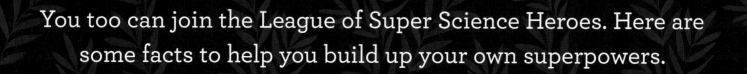

GLOSSARY OF TERMS

ATOM

Atoms are tiny units of mass (a million times smaller than one of your hairs). They are the building blocks of all things. The word atom means "indivisible" because it was once believed that they were so small, they could never be divided.

CHEMISTRY

Chemistry is a science that studies the properties of atoms. For instance, how atoms connect with each other to make molecules, and how atoms and molecules come together to create other substances.

INTERNATIONAL COMMISSION FOR INTELLECTUAL COOPERATION

The International Commission for Intellectual Cooperation is an organization established in 1922 that helps scientists around the world exchange information and research.

LABORATORY

A laboratory is a room or building that has specific equipment used to carry out scientific research and experiments.

MATHEMATICS

Mathematics is the study of logical thinking, numbers, and shapes. It describes numerical operations (like adding and subtracting), as well as how numbers can be used to solve problems.

LEAGUE OF NATIONS

The League of Nations is an organization created by many countries in 1920 with the goal of maintaining world peace.

RADIOGRAPHY

Radiography is a technique that creates an image of something using X-rays. It's very useful to help us see things we cannot see with just our eyes (like your bones).

NOBEL PRIZE

The Nobel Prize is a very important prize given once a year to people who have made important contributions to the fields of literature, medicine, physics, chemistry, peace, and economics.

PHYSICS

Physics is the study of energy and matter through space and time. The word "physics" comes from Ancient Greek and it means "knowledge of nature." The primary goal of physics is to understand how the universe behaves.

POLONIUM

Polonium (Po, atomic number 84) is a highly radioactive substance discovered because of the rays it emits. It is very toxic. This element was named after Poland, Marie Curie's country of birth.

RADIUM

Radium (Ra, atomic number 88) is a highly radioactive material that can cause radioluminescence (it can make other materials give off light). This element is named after the sun.

RADIOACTIVE

A nucleus is the heart of an atom. If an atom starts to fall apart, it sends out energy in the form of rays. Radioactivity is the process by which the nucleus loses its energy.

MARIE CURIE TIMELINE

Maria graduates from high school with a gold medal

Marie becomes the first female faculty member at the École Normale Supérieure

NOV. 7, 1867:
Maria Skłodowska is born

1883 **1891** **1893** **1894** **1898** **1900**

Maria moves to Paris and changes her name to Marie when she enrolls in the Sorbonne

Marie receives a degree in physics

Marie publishes a paper coining the term "radioactivity"

Marie and Pierre publish a paper announcing the existence of polonium, named in honor of her home country, Poland

Marie receives a degree in mathematics

Marie and Pierre publish a paper announcing the existence of radium, named after the Latin word for "rays"

Marie, Pierre, and Henri Becquerel receive the Nobel Prize in Physics

Marie receives the Nobel Prize in Chemistry

Marie and several colleagues create the Curie Foundation, which becomes an international force in the treatment of cancer

1903 **1906** **1910** **1911** **1914** **1920**

JULY 4, 1934: Marie dies

Pierre dies

Marie's fundamental Treatise on Radioactivity is published, a classic two-volume work on radioactivity research

Marie founds the Radium Institute, now called the Curie Institute

Marie becomes the first female faculty professor of general physics at the Sorbonne

MORE ABOUT MARIE CURIE:

Marie Curie and Albert Einstein were pen pals!

Marie Curie's daughter, Irene Joliot-Curie, also won a Nobel Prize in Chemistry (1935).

Marie Curie drove an ambulance during the war and helped thousands of wounded soldiers and civilians.

During the war, Marie offered to donate her two gold medals to support the war effort.

THE IMPACT OF MARIE CURIE'S DISCOVERIES—OR HOW SHE SAVED THE DAY!

Marie Curie's discoveries were very important in many respects.

• The discovery of radium made it possible to create X-ray machines and provide radiation therapy. Both can be very useful in helping us get better when we're sick.

• The discovery of radium helped scientists unlock important secrets about atoms, and understand more about the world around us and how we are made.

• Marie Curie grew up in a time when women did not have many opportunities to study, work, or do important research. By persisting, she became a role model for other women, making it possible for them to also study, work, and do remarkable research.

RESOURCES

To learn more about Marie Curie and her research, visit these websites.*

American Institute of Physics:
https://history.aip.org/history/exhibits/curie/contents.htm

BBC Podcast: "A Pioneering Life":
http://www.bbc.co.uk/programmes/p04vx744

YouTube documentaries:
https://www.youtube.com/watch?v=do41AJwIjZE
https://www.youtube.com/watch?v=3HH_4D1V2rE

Nobel Prize biography:
http://www.nobelprize.org/nobel_prizes/physics/laureates/1903/marie-curie-bio.html

Science websites:
https://www.famousscientists.org/marie-curie
https://britannica.com/biography/Marie-Curie
http://www.21sci-tech.com/articles/wint02–03/MarieSklodowskaCurie.html

*Don't forget to ask you parents' permission anytime you visit a website!

KARLA VALENTI is a writer of children's picture books and middle grade novels. Originally from Mexico, Karla has lived in many places she now calls home. Most recently she and her brood of budding superheroes have put down roots in the Chicagoland area. You can find out more at karlavalenti.com.

ANNALISA BEGHELLI graduated from the IUAV University of Venice in 2006 with a degree in architecture, and worked in a Milan design studio for four years before pursuing her passion as a freelance illustrator. In 2011, she received a master's degree in publishing illustration from Mimaster, and in 2017 she founded consultant design studio FAI31. Visit her at annalisabeghelli.com.

MICAELA CRESPO QUESADA was a persistent super science hero herself back in the day! She has lived in five different countries, has a PhD in chemical engineering, and was a recipient of a Marie Skłodowska Curie Fellowship in 2014, which she spent in Cambridge, UK, studying all things solar fuels. She now lives in Switzerland where she raises two super science heroes of her own and is passionate about showing them—and all other children!—how they don't need superpowers in order to achieve great things.